Sleeping Beauty–
100 Years Later

by Laura North and Gary Northfield

Crabtree Publishing Company

www.crabtreebooks.com

Crabtree Publishing Company
www.crabtreebooks.com
1-800-387-7650

PMB 59051, 350 Fifth Ave.
59th Floor,
New York, NY 10118

616 Welland Ave.
St. Catharines, ON
L2M 5V6

Published by Crabtree Publishing in 2014

For Paul – L.N.

Series editor: Melanie Palmer
Editor: Crystal Sikkens
Notes to adults: Reagan Miller
Series advisor: Catherine Glavina
Series designer: Peter Scoulding
**Production coordinator and
    Prepress technician:** Margaret Amy Salter
Print coordinator: Margaret Amy Salter

Text © Laura North 2010
Illustrations © Gary Northfield 2010

First published in 2010
by Franklin Watts
(A division of Hachette
Children's Books)

Printed in
Canada/022014/MA20131220

**Library and Archives Canada
Cataloguing in Publication**

North, Laura, author
       Sleeping beauty--100 years later / written by
Laura North ; illustrated by Gary Northfield.

(Tadpoles: fairytale twists)
Issued in print and electronic formats.
ISBN 978-0-7787-0444-7 (bound).--ISBN 978-0-7787-
0479-9 (pbk.).--ISBN 978-1-4271-7564-9 (pdf).--ISBN
978-1-4271-7556-4 (html)

       I. Northfield, Gary, 1969-, illustrator II. Title.

PZ7.N815Sl 2014   j823'.92   C2013-908323-5
                                       C2013-908324-3

**Library of Congress
Cataloging-in-Publication Data**

CIP available at Library of Congress

This story is based on the traditional fairy tale,
Sleeping Beauty, but with a new twist.
Can you make up your own twist for the story?

A long time ago,

a king and queen had

a beautiful baby daughter.

"Let's have a big party to celebrate," said the King. They invited everyone in the kingdom.

HAPPY BIRTH

But they forgot to invite
one fairy.

She burst into the party in a rage. "I curse your daughter! She will cut her finger and fall asleep for a hundred years. Only a prince can wake her!"

"That will teach them to forget me!" she thought as she flew away.

The King and Queen were terrified.
"No sharp things!" screamed
the Queen, taking the knife
and fork away.

"No playing outdoors!" said the King. The Princess wasn't allowed to do anything. She was miserable.

When the Princess reached her
18th birthday, the King and Queen
let her wander around the castle.

She found a room with an old
spinning wheel.

The Princess was curious.

She tried making some thread

on the spinning wheel.

"Ouch!" she cried. She had pricked her finger on the needle. Suddenly, she fell into a deep sleep.

Everyone else fell asleep, too!
Years passed. Cobwebs
covered the castle.

One hundred years
later, a prince wearing
sunglasses drove up to the castle.

He talked on a cell phone.

He listened to music in earphones.

He wore jeans. A lot had changed
while the Princess had been asleep!

The Prince found the Princess.
"What a sleeping beauty!" he
thought. He went over and
kissed her.

"Are you my Prince, my true love?"
asked the Princess, waking up.
"Just call me Harry," said the Prince.
"I'd like to take you on a date."

"A date?" said the Princess.

"I wonder what that is!"

Harry took her outside.

Everything looked so different!

"Is this your carriage? Where
is the horse?" asked the Princess.
"No need for one of those!" said
Harry, starting the car engine.

"Let's go to the amusement park,"
Harry said. The Princess whizzed
around and upside down on a
roller coaster. "I've never had so
much fun!" she screamed.

Harry gave her a single red rose.

A thorn on the rose cut her finger.

"Oh no, what will happen to me now?" cried the Princess. "Will I fall asleep for another 100 years?"

27

"No, here's a Band-Aid," said Harry, and he stuck it on her finger.

The Princess smiled. Life was so much better 100 years later!

Put these pictures in the correct order. Which event is the most important? Try writing the story in your own words. Use your imagination to put your own "twist" on the story!

Puzzle 2

Match the speech bubbles to the correct character in the story. Turn the page to check your answers.

Notes for adults

TADPOLES: Fairytale Twists are engaging, imaginative stories designed for early fluent readers. The books may also be used for read-alouds or shared reading with young children.

TADPOLES: Fairytale Twists are humorous stories with a unique twist on traditional fairy tales. Each story can be compared to the original fairy tale, or appreciated on its own. Fairy tales are a key type of literary text found in the Common Core State Standards.

THE FOLLOWING PROMPTS BEFORE, DURING, AND AFTER READING SUPPORT LITERACY SKILL DEVELOPMENT AND CAN ENRICH SHARED READING EXPERIENCES:

1. **Before Reading**: Do a picture walk through the book, previewing the illustrations. Ask the reader to predict what will happen in the story. For example, ask the reader what he or she thinks the twist in the story will be.

2. **During Reading**: Encourage the reader to use context clues and illustrations to determine the meaning of unknown words or phrases.

3. **During Reading**: Have the reader stop midway through the book to revisit his or her predictions. Does the reader wish to change his or her predictions based on what they have read so far?

4. **During and After Reading**: Encourage the reader to make different connections:
   Text-to-Text: How is this story similar to/different from other stories you have read?
   Text-to-World: How are events in this story similar to/different from things that happen in the real world?
   Text-to-Self: Does a character or event in this story remind you of anything in your own life?

5. **After Reading**: Encourage the child to reread the story and to retell it using his or her own words. Invite the child to use the illustrations as a guide.

HERE ARE OTHER TITLES FROM TADPOLES: FAIRYTALE TWISTS FOR YOU TO ENJOY:

Cinderella's Big Foot	978-0-7787-0440-9 RLB	978-0-7787-0448-5 PB
Jack and the Bean Pie	978-0-7787-0441-6 RLB	978-0-7787-0449-2 PB
Little Bad Riding Hood	978-0-7787-0442-3 RLB	978-0-7787-0450-8 PB
Princess Frog	978-0-7787-0443-0 RLB	978-0-7787-0452-2 PB
The Lovely Duckling	978-0-7787-0445-4 RLB	978-0-7787-0480-5 PB
The Princess and the Frozen Peas	978-0-7787-0446-1 RLB	978-0-7787-0481-2 PB
The Three Little Pigs and the New Neighbor	978-0-7787-0447-8 RLB	978-0-7787-0482-9 PB

VISIT WWW.CRABTREEBOOKS.COM FOR OTHER CRABTREE BOOKS.

Answers
Puzzle 1
The correct order is: 1e, 2d, 3f, 4a, 5c, 6b

Puzzle 2
The Princess: 1, 4
Harry: 2, 5
The bad fairy: 3, 6